W9-AAL-962

If I Ran the Family

LEE and SUE KAISER JOHNSON

Illustrated by Roberta Collier Morales

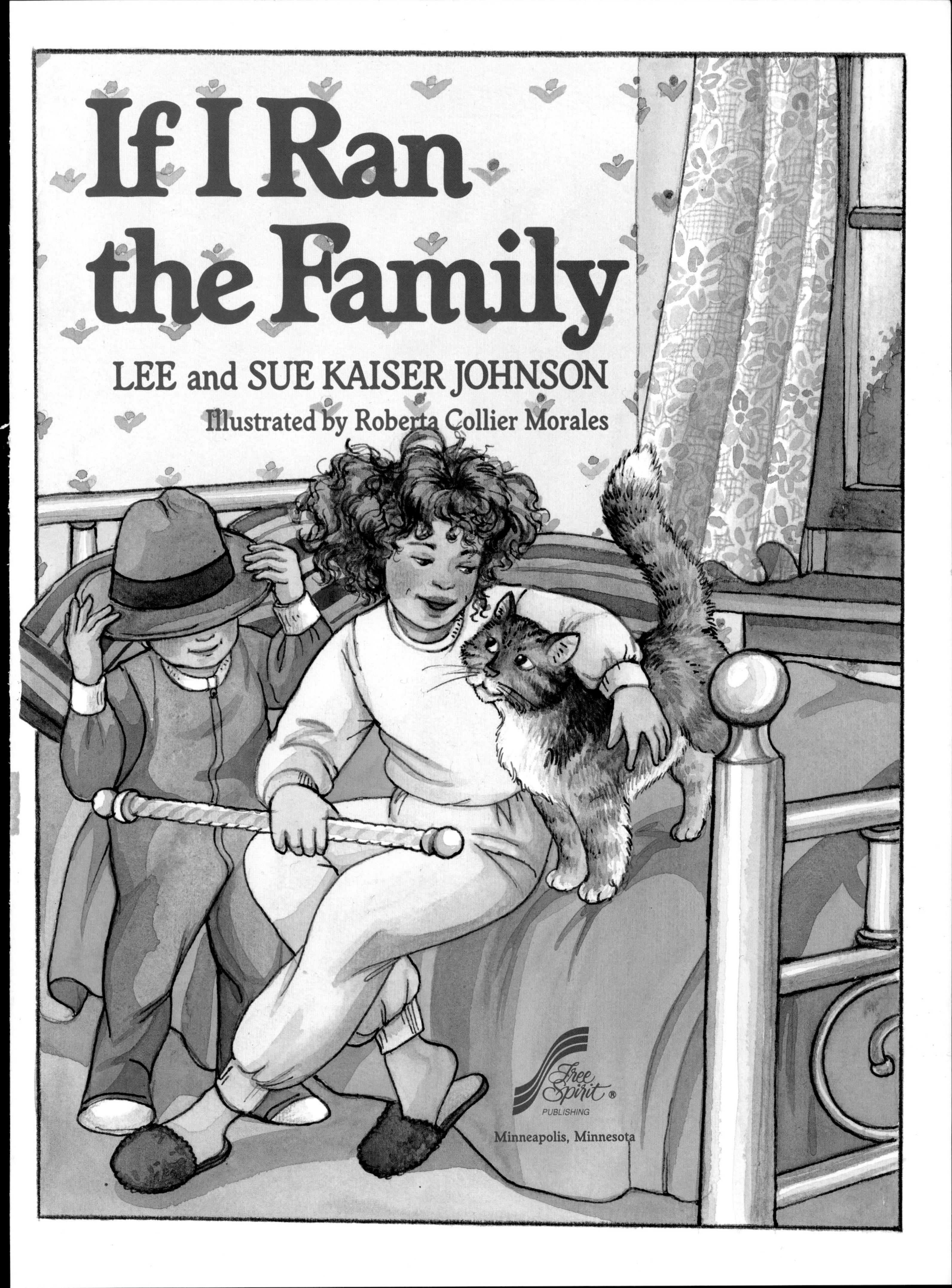

Free Spirit® PUBLISHING

Minneapolis, Minnesota

Dedication

To our children,
Andrea, Eric, and Ellie,
without whom this book would never have come to be.

-L.& S.K.J.

To all children who know how important it is to speak out and be heard.

-R.C.M.

Library of Congress Cataloging-in-Publication Data
Kaiser Johnson, Lee, 1962-
If I ran the family / by Lee and Sue Kaiser Johnson ; edited by Pamela Espeland.
p. cm.
Summary: Debbie Dundee imagines living in a family run according to her way, in which everyone is free to express his/her feelings regardless of what they are.
ISBN 0-915793-41-5
[1. Family life—Fiction. 2. Emotions—Fiction. 3. Self-acceptance—Fiction. 4. Stories in rhyme.] I. Kaiser Johnson, Sue, 1963- II. Espeland, Pamela, 1951- . III. Title.
PZ8.3.K1245If 1992
[E]—dc20 92-948
CIP
AC

10 9 8 7 6 5 4 3 2 1

Edited by Pamela Espeland
Book design and production supervision by MacLean & Tuminelly

The illustrations are done in color pencil and Windsor Newton transparent watercolors on heavyweight illustration paper.
The text type is set in ITC Usherwood, composed by MacLean & Tuminelly.
The display type is set in Worchester Round.
Color separations are made by Bright Arts (Hong Kong) Ltd.
Printed and bound by Sing Cheong Printing Co. Ltd., Hong Kong.

Free Spirit Publishing Inc.
400 First Avenue North, Suite 616
Minneapolis, Minnesota 55401
U.S.A.
(612) 338-2068

Foreword

Although in real life families need to be run by grownups, not children, we adults don't have to do that job alone! We can be alert to the needs of our children and do our part to see that children get those needs met.

If I Ran the Family can help us do that. The needs of the Dundee children — and all families, I believe — are engagingly presented by the spirited young Debbie Dundee. Without a command, a shame, or a blame, Debbie reminds children and parents that all kids need to know when to seek comfort, to share and not stuff feelings, to say no to unwanted touch, to avoid troublesome secrets, and to make their needs known.

Lee and Sue Kaiser Johnson offer adults as well as children a boost toward a healthy, democratic family in a book that deserves to be read and enjoyed many, many times.

Jean Illsley Clarke, author of *Self-Esteem: A Family Affair* and *Growing Up Again*

"Now you'd probably think,"
said young Debbie Dundee,
"that my family's as great
as a family can be.
(And to look from the outside,
I'd have to agree.)
But if I ran the family,
if I had my say,
if I were the grownup,
just for one day,
then we'd all find out
how our family could be,
if running the family
were left up to me!

"I think that today
I'll try it and see....

“The first thing I’ll do,
now that I have my way,
is to make sure we all
have some say-so each day.
In my sort of family,
we all have a voice.
When problems come up,
we all have a choice.

"And when problems do happen,
I'm glad to report
that my family is
the most comforting sort.
If you're riding your bike
and you swallow a bug,
or you skin your left knee
on the living-room rug,
you can have a good cry
and a long, tender hug.

Why, you can cry puddles!
You can cry lakes!
It's okay to cry
for as long as it takes.
We'll bring out a bucket.
We'll bring out a mop!
You'll decide for yourself
when you're ready to stop.
Because bad things can happen
to sniffled-back tears.

"They might make you angry,
or turn into fears,
or you could end up
with a stomach that aches.
You might even hit
someone else by mistake!
So no one will try
to make you 'be good'
or say, 'Big kids don't cry,'
because sometimes they should!

"When you're all through crying
and your eyes are still wet,
if you need a big hug,
why, a hug's what you'll get,
the warmest, most snug,
and cuddly hug yet.
The best kind of hug
that can only be freed
by someone who gets
all the hugs that they need.

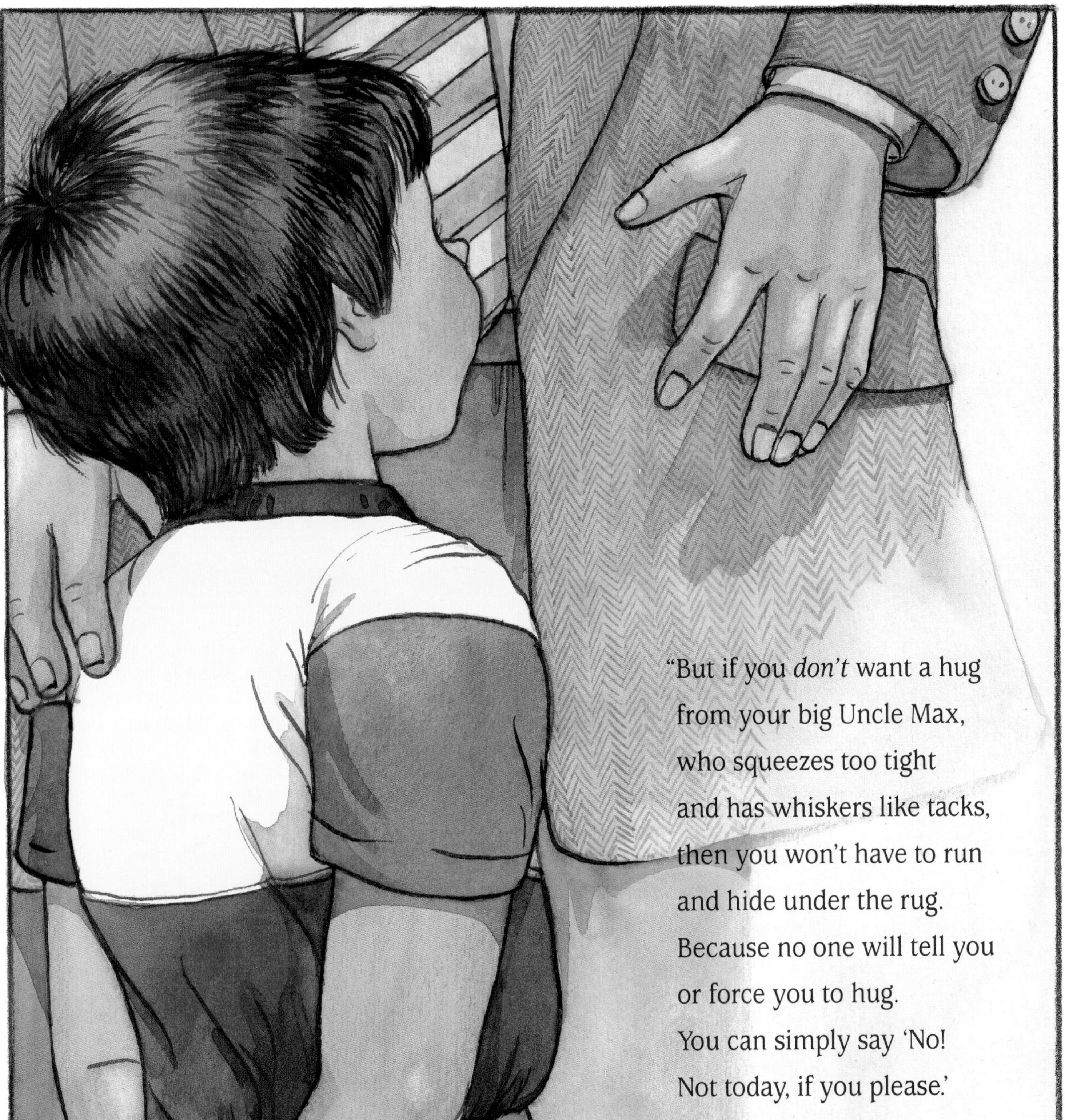

"But if you *don't* want a hug
from your big Uncle Max,
who squeezes too tight
and has whiskers like tacks,
then you won't have to run
and hide under the rug.
Because no one will tell you
or force you to hug.
You can simply say 'No!
Not today, if you please.'
And no one will frown,
or holler, or tease.
You can say how you feel
and not have to fake it.
Saying 'No' is okay!
This family can take it!

"As long as we're going
to tell how we feel,
let's shine a bright light
on this 'keep secret' deal.
A secret, some say,
must be kept locked inside.
A secret, they say,
is something to hide.

“Well, here’s the new rule
for this family of mine:
Some things you can choose
not to share, and that’s fine.
But you don’t have to fall for
that TOP SECRET line!
If you have a secret,
you *can* let it out.
Everything can be shared,
everything talked about.
You can always share freely
with someone you trust.
In the family Dundee,
this rule is a must!

"Though the truth might be scary,
it's time to make clear
that there's nothing more normal
than feeling some fear.
How about that dark basement,
with its damp, musty smell?

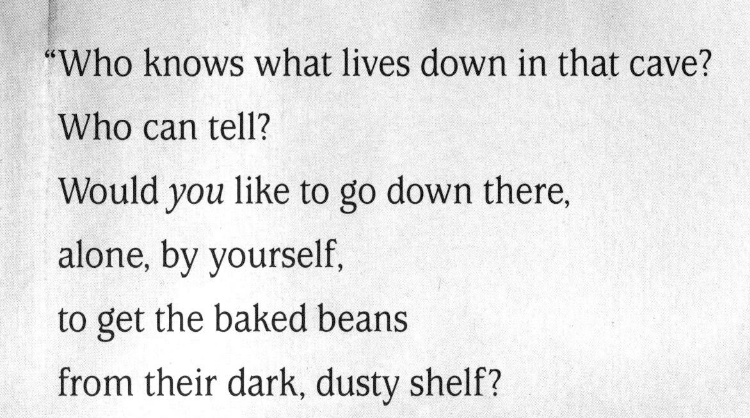

“Who knows what lives down in that cave?
Who can tell?
Would *you* like to go down there,
alone, by yourself,
to get the baked beans
from their dark, dusty shelf?

“Well, the next thing we’ll do
is make that place bright.
Six hundred huge light bulbs
sounds just about right.

"And we'll hold your hand tight
and go with you downstairs,
until you feel braver
and have no more cares,
until you are quite sure
the basement is home,
until you feel safe
to be downstairs alone.

“All this talk makes me hungry,
so let’s take a look
at the family kitchen,
where I’m the head cook!
Do you ever sit down
at the table and wait
for that big, ugly fish
to flip off of your plate?

"How about those chopped livers
or steamed Brussels sprouts
or that new casserole
you don't want to 'try out'?
For those foods that you hate,
do you ever wish
you could say, 'Thanks, but no thanks,'
and just pass the dish?

“Well, today is your luckiest
three-meal day,
because in this family
you have the say!
You get to pick
what to eat or to skip,
if you want second helpings
or a big double dip.

"But if corned-beef-and-cabbage
makes you turn green,
you don't have to eat it
or lick your plate clean.
You can make your own choices
without making a scene.

"And if there's a time
when you don't want to play,
or you don't feel like smiling,
it's really okay!
In our family, if anyone
feels like a grump,
it's all right to say,
'Hey, I'm down in the dumps!'

"They can say it out loud.
They can speak for themselves.
But they *don't* get to blame it
on anyone else!
We can all understand
why they're grumbling along
and we don't have to think
that *we've* done something wrong.

“How you feel inside
is just right for you.
That’s true for all kids
and for all grownups, too.

“No matter your feeling,
no matter your mood,
there’s nothing that *is*
that can make you less good.

"Now you've heard my story
if just for one day,
I ran the family
and had things my way.
I know that I'm twenty-some
years in advance,
and I'll just have to wait
in line for my chance.

“If you stick around,
someday you’ll see
the changes I’ll make,”
said young Debbie Dundee,
“when running the family
is left up to me.

“But what about *your* house?
Do *you* have a say?
What are *your* rights
in your family today?
Do grownups and kids
get respected the same?
Or when something goes wrong,
do kids get the blame?

"Can you share all your feelings
without any fear?
When you want a hug,
can you hold someone near?
When you need to talk,
is there someone to hear?
Can you just be yourself
from morning to night
and not always be perfect,
and nice, and polite?

"Now that you're thinking
how *your* family could be,
will you share what you know?
Will you tell what you see?
You have the power
to say what you need
and make your wants known
without taking the lead.
You don't have to wait
until you have your way.
You can start making choices
beginning today!"